RIDGEBACK TALES

Legba's Magic Mark
Everybody Loves Shep
The Dog Wife

M ICHAEL H OFFMAN

ISBN: 978-1-5356-0125-2

Dedication

RIDGEBACK TALES HONORS JANE AND Cory Bowers, breeders of champion-quality Rhodesian Ridgebacks at CJS Ranch in Wildomar, California. Since 2000, American Kennel Club judges nationwide have given CJS Ranch dogs top show honors for their remarkably confident gait and powerful conformational structure. Everyone who purchases a dog from CJS Ranch benefits from Jane and Cory's active mentorship in raising and training these fine animals. I purchased my male livernose Ridgeback, Mister Brown, at CJS Ranch in 2012, and he earned his AKC Champion status before the age of two. He's bold enough to face Africa's most dangerous game and gentle enough to walk my granddaughter home from school.

Michael Hoffman, Dr.AD
Dana Point, CA

Contents

Legba's Magic Mark

WAY BACK ON THE VAST grassy plains of Africa, Thunder reigned as king of the elephants. He stood majestic as a great grey mountain, but he had a problem. Lions and more lions and even more lions prowled in the brush, hungry for plump baby elephants. Sometimes the aggressive lions even bit at the mother elephants' trunks when they shielded their babies. It was a terrible and dangerous situation.

So Thunder lifted his trunk high and trumpeted to summon his friend Tsavo, the king of the big, brave brown dogs. Thunder told Tsavo he needed help scaring the lions away. Tsavo and his mates were helpful friends, and they had tangled with lions many times before.

The plan was for all the big, brave brown dogs to crouch unseen between the legs of the bull elephants, and when the lions closed in to attack the baby elephants and their mothers, the dogs would explode out in fierce surprise and challenge the lions' might and manes. Thunder sweetened the deal with a reward by promising to let the big, brave brown dogs sleep in the cool shade between the bull elephants' legs any time they wanted to escape the heat of the sun. It was a very good deal for the dogs.

The next day dawned hot and windy, and the air carried the scent of baby elephants right into all the lions' noses. Many, many great tawny lions slunk through the brush, forming a circle of teeth and claws and growls around the elephants. The baby elephants huddled close to their mothers, while all the big, brave brown dogs peered out silently from between the bull elephants' legs.

As the lions crept ever closer, Tsavo whispered to Thunder,

"You have nothing to fear. This is the day the lions stop bullying the elephants once and for all. I promise!"

Thunder told Tsavo,

"I trust you, brother. When I can see the lions' eyes glinting and their dark manes hovering in the thick brush, I will wiggle my ears, and then you..."

No sooner had Thunder said that than Maluku the tawny lion king rushed in with his huge black mane bristling. Thunder raised his trunk and trumpeted and wiggled his ears and all the big, brave brown dogs rushed like a furious wave from their hiding place between the bull elephants' legs.

Maluku didn't know what was happening. Suddenly dogs attacked on all sides with cunning ferocity. Like a wave of angry brown danger they growled and snapped, batting his face with their heavy paws and biting holes in his haunches and shoulders, then leaping away to escape his massive paws. Maluku spun in narrowing circles but couldn't get away. More and more dogs rushed out from beneath their elephant hiding places and trapped the other lions in a prison of fearless teeth.

The big, brave brown dogs were smart. They knew a six-hundred-pound lion like Maluku could easily kill any dog, but was helpless when four or more attacked in unison, diving in and leaping back in a constant furious ballet. Tsavo and his mates continued to circle and bark and bite until the exhausted Maluku feared his end was near. He bellowed a deep-throated retreat growl, warning the other lions to back off. The dogs watched as the lions started slinking away one by one, all bitten, humiliated, and bloody.

When all the lions had vanished into the distant brush and all the baby elephants were safe, Thunder told Tsavo he had a great surprise for him and his brave friends.

"Come, my loyal friends. You are hot, thirsty, dirty, and tired. We will reward your bravery."

Thunder and the bull elephants formed a great long line and rose up on their hind legs, trumpeting thank you to the big, brave brown dogs. The bull elephants invited all the dogs to come rest in the shade between their legs to cool off.

Tsavo was the first dog to accept the offer. As he lay between Thunder's legs, the great elephant king reached his massive trunk down and rubbed it ever so gently up and down Tsavo's back. He squirted water on Tsavo's back to clean away the dirt and grime until it was slick and cool and clean. Then he gave Tsavo a long, deep drink from his huge trunk.

Tsavo had never met with such kindness. He fell into a deep, well-deserved sleep. The other bull elephants tended to each and every dog, rubbing and cleaning and sheltering them until every one was clean and fast asleep. All that long African night, the big, brave brown dogs dreamed in unison of their victory and of their new elephant friends.

"Our bravery will be legend. We will protect all our friends, and we will always show our loyalty to those who need us. That's what makes us big, brave brown dogs."

Tsavo was the first to wake up in the morning. He stretched and yawned his sleep away and stepped out into the cool sunrise. One by one all the other big, brave brown dogs woke up too and gathered together to share stories of their victory over the lions. They felt unusually bold and cocky, and bragged and licked each other in congratulations.

In their excitement, they also noticed something different about the fur on each other's backs. Tsavo inspected each dog and sure enough, every single one had changed overnight. He asked Thunder if he knew anything about it.

"Thunder, my tall grey friend. What has happened to us? Our coats all have this strange new mark. It's not a scar. It doesn't hurt. In fact, it's very bold looking. It makes the hyena's bristly back look just plain ugly."

Thunder knew the answer, but he never told Tsavo. It was to remain a profound mystery for all the animals to marvel at in the ages to come. Knowing the dogs should be grandly rewarded, Thunder had called the African Trickster god Legba to come put a blessing mark on their backs during the long sleepy night. As the strongest of all the Nature gods, Legba agreed to use his magic touch to transform the already brave dogs into a brand-new animal, the African Lion Hound. Legba made his mark in the shape of a bold ridge on the same spot where the bull elephants had rubbed and rinsed and cleaned the dogs so kindly the day before.

Since that magical night and forevermore, the hair of each hound's back grows in the opposite direction to form a bold, wide ridge of slick, stout hair with delicate feathered brows along the edges. Starting wide right between the shoulder blades, it narrows gracefully to a point just above the hips, like an elegant arrow. The ridge is a comrade's badge of courage. On the great morning of their new life, all the big, brave brown African Lion Hounds barked and leapt high in the air and ran around showing off their ridges to each other, making hound talk all day long… and that is how the Ridgeback got his ridge.

Everybody Loves Shep

THE NEWLY MADE AFRICAN LION Hound Tsavo was so proud of his ridge that he asked the Nature god Legba how he could repay the favor. Legba pondered for a moment, like gods always do, then said,

> *"You are a loyal mbwa [dog]. I will grant you many lifetimes if you promise to share your unselfish love with human beings. And as you love men, you will become legendary for your kindness and intelligence."*

Tsavo didn't understand the idea of reincarnation, but he agreed, the way helpful hounds always do.

Many seasons of sun and rain passed, and Tsavo's broad, strong muzzle turned grey. His forechest sank, and his sinewy haunches lost their spring. Every day he rested in the shade of Thunder the elephant king's legs. They reminisced about the day they defeated the lion king Maluku and his snarling pride.

One day Tsavo couldn't stand up. Thunder rubbed and comforted him with his dexterous trunk as musical tones rose from deep inside Tsavo's chest. These magical notes were his last-ever hound talk. Tsavo talked with faster and faster breaths and said kwaheri (goodbye) to Thunder. Then he let out one long, deep breath as his spirit left his body. Part of it rose high into the air like crystalline smoke and part turned into rich green water and sank into the ground. All the elephants circled around Tsavo's still body, rose up on their hind legs with trunks held high, and trumpeted a farewell salute that all the animals could hear.

Far off in the tall grass, Maluku the lion king hung his head and said a farewell to Tsavo. He felt blessed to have met and battled such a fine mwba dog. Like Tsavo, Maluku had lived long enough. On slow, tired legs he found a hiding place under an ancient baobab tree. He lay down and left his brave body, too.

One thousand years later, rescue workers at the 9/11 disaster site in New York City marveled at a Rhodesian Ridgeback S.A.R. dog named Rafiki. His handler, David, said that name meant friend in Swahili, but all the workers insisted on calling him Shep, an American name. He looked like a perfectly sculpted statue, with striking, heroic proportions. At age three, he weighed over one hundred and ten pounds. His forelegs resembled pillars, and his graceful neck arched high and thick. His loins bulged with muscles like steel cords and his deep forechest rose and fell like a bellows.

Shep's agility seemed impossible for an animal his size. His movements showed more elegance and feral determination than the other S.A.R. dogs'. He floated over the hot rubble with an intensely focused lope, never stumbling or mis-stepping. Rescue work had awakened the fearless fluid intelligence of Shep's ancient hunting DNA. His first life as Tsavo on the African veldt could not be denied.

Shep worked two days on and one day off, ignoring intense heat, smoke, and razor-sharp glass and metal. No matter how much smoky dust clouded his eyes, Shep never stopped looking, sniffing, and digging. He refused to sleep anywhere but underneath a grey Red Cross hospital trailer. It reminded him of the shelter his great ancestor Tsavo once found between the legs of the elephant king Thunder.

Shep found thirty-seven people. Only six still lived, but Shep treated them all with the same enthusiasm. He nuzzled and licked and made musical hound talk, trying to awaken even those who were already gone. This was his way of blessing them.

> *"If you cannot waken, goodbye. Travel safe over the Rainbow Bridge."*

The firemen called him the "African Loving Hound" instead of the African Lion Hound. When David commanded him out of the rubble at the end of each work shift, Shep strained against his harness, looking back over his shoulder and whining. David understood exactly what Shep was saying:

> *"No, I'm not done yet. I can hear more people. Can't you hear them? They want me to come back. Let me keep looking, please!"*

Shep wasn't immune to stress and depression on days when he couldn't find any survivors. When the day's search came up empty, David would send another fireman to go hide in the wreckage where Shep could easily find him. David always suspected that Shep knew this game, but Shep's delighted barks made him forget the ruse. Shep's happiness mattered more.

David retired when the search work ended and adopted Shep. The resilient dog had no symptoms of the post-traumatic stress disorder that left some S.A.R. canines unsuited for a second life as pets. Man and dog retired to a comfortable life by a wide grassy park in a small Southern California town. The long warm days reminded Shep of another warm place, but he couldn't remember exactly where that was. He quickly became the neighborhood's favorite dog. Children and mothers alike delighted in his impressive stature and gentle nature. When a new family moved into the neighborhood, David introduced them to Shep, explained his 9/11 background, and assured parents of his dependability.

On school days, Shep waited for the school bus so he could greet the children and escort them across the park to their front doors. He had already kept the ancient promise he'd made to Legba in his Tsavo incarnation by helping humans at 9/11, and he took shepherding these children just as seriously. He wagged his tail and kissed each and every child stepping down off the bus, making excited hound talk.

"Hello, hello, my little friends. I am so happy to see you. Let me walk you home to your family. You are safe with me."

Life with Shep was good for the children, and David watched proudly from his doorstep as Shep performed his task.

One drizzly afternoon Shep sat patiently in the wet, waiting for the bus. The sprinkling grew into hard, steady rain. The children piled off the bus and started running home as fast as they could in the downpour. The newest and smallest boy, Mikey, slipped stepping down off the bus and fell face first in the mud. Shep hadn't met Mikey yet, but that didn't matter. Shep knew fear when he saw it, and he knew exactly what to do. He pushed his strong muzzle into the mud and lifted Mikey up on his feet. Mikey took hold of Shep's collar with his tiny hands. Boy and dog started walking as fast as they could toward Mikey's house. Shep shook rainwater off his shoulders with mighty shakes, and Mikey wiped water from his eyes.

Suddenly a lightning bolt exploded, filling the sky and bathing the park in an eerie green-white glow. The thundercrack that followed shook the ground and sent Shep into instinctive survival mode. He remembered some great beast somewhere back in time telling him that lightning storms could be deadly. He bolted forward, and the sudden movement trapped Mikey's hand in his collar. Shep sprinted toward the boy's house as the collar pinched tighter, drawing blood. Shep stopped once to lick Mikey's wound, then ran again with Mikey bouncing off his shoulder like a rag doll.

Mikey's mother stood panicking in the storm outside her front door. She could hear Mikey's screams between booms of thunder, but could not see anything through the heavy rain. Suddenly Shep appeared out of the darkness with Mikey hanging twisted and bloody from the collar. Shep lay down in the water, craning his head back and biting and clawing with his hind legs to break the collar and set the boy free. He remembered again his ancient duty:

"Keeping this little boy safe is the whole reason I am here."

Mikey's mother knelt down and tried to untangle her son, but only tightened the tangle. Mikey fell unconscious, and Shep winced and barked loudly at the pain. There wasn't going to be any life-saving 911 phone call for this chaos. Mikey's father had witnessed the entire scene from his kitchen window. He grabbed his shotgun from the hall closet, stepped out into the rain, put the barrel to Shep's head, and pulled the trigger.

Shep yelped once and lay quivering in the wet grass as Mikey's father released the collar and rushed his son into the house. David emerged through the rain and fell to his knees, cradling Shep's head. He felt the great tawny body vibrate as its soul broke free from the flesh. Pulsating waves of the deepest blue, green, and yellow light poured from Shep's forehead and rose into the air to form a rainbow arch over the scene. The faintest sound of African djembe drums seemed to rise from the earth. David stared into Shep's deep golden eyes and heard his beloved companion's final message:

"I must go now, but don't worry. You and I have been together many times before, and so we will again. I was Tsavo, then Rafiki, and now Shep, just as you have been and will be many men. There is a rainbow bridge between the

lives of men and dogs. One day we will meet there and speak of our great adventures. But until then, kwaheri, goodbye."

Years passed as David thought about the safe place he and Shep had created for one another in an often-cruel world. He wondered why the hearts of men could not love unconditionally like Shep's. It was just the Rhodesian Ridgeback way, as simple as that. That kind of love was too unselfish for humans to grasp.

David had always wanted to be a writer, but when he became a family man, he had opted for the security of a firefighter's career. He hadn't written a word for years, but one day as he sat at Shep's grave, words poured spontaneously from his heart. He could hear Shep tell the story of his soul's great adventure.

He took up his old interest in writing short stories and poems. He always favored the one Shep asked him to write that day, a story sent from beyond the Rainbow Bridge. It wrote itself like music.

Shep's Lucky Day

My boy Shep
breaks the joy barrier
with his ears pinned back
his tongue a pink flag of bliss
strong feet barely touching the grass
as he sprints after the same elusive dove
he has chased across the chaos of fields and wind
since the first beast ran.

I try to follow
but he leaps effortlessly into the air
shapeshifting before my eyes
part animal, part angel, part my love
a lightning bolt of the pure inexplicable joy
we all desire.

Poised in wind
Shep cries out to the dove
take me with you
I have to see what's there
on the other side.

Then Shep looks back at me
his golden eyes remembering
how much he will miss
our warm fireside at evening
but his trusting eyes still implore
Is it OK if I go now?
Oh, please let me learn to fly.

I can only stand there speechless
as his scent fills the air
and he slowly fades from view
because of course I know
my boy Shep has left me;
he has already gone
into the light.

The Dog Wife

A KIND OLD MAN LIVED in a clean white house at the edge of town by a wide green field. The circus made its home in the field for two weeks every spring. The man always watched in amazement while the roustabouts scurried around erecting gigantic red, white, and blue tents. In just a few hours the empty field turned into a magic playground.

The old man made sure to be first in line at the ticket window every day. When the gates to the midway swung open, he rushed in like a child at Christmas. He feasted his eyes and ears on the wondrous animals, the bright face paint of the laughing clowns, and the beautiful girls on the "Darlings of the Amazon" stage. His heart beat fast with youthful curiosity as he handed in his tickets to see the "World's Fattest Horse" and tried to win a giant stuffed panda by throwing a ping-pong ball into a glass of water. He laughed when he missed and the carnival man working the booth laughed, too.

The circus' intoxicating sights and sounds made the old man forget his loneliness. Long ago, his beautiful young wife had grown gravely ill. No medicine could save her, and neither could his deep and true devotion to their love. One morning she told him it was time for her to go. She whispered in his ear,

"This is not the end for us. You will find me again in another body in another place, but be careful until that day. Many bogus lovers will try to steal your heart. Wait for me. My love will keep you safe."

Then, with a sweet last breath that smelled of roses and honey, she stopped living in her beautiful human body. Her soul rose up into the air like silver mist as she grew still in his arms.

He dared a few times to seek her in the form of another woman, only to be betrayed. The search wearied him but also made him wiser. He learned to recognize the masquerade of imposters, their too-eagerness, their flirtiness, and their effusive promises of everlasting love that never came true. He finally resigned himself to dying without ever finding her. He lived reclusively, filling his days with study of esoteric, soulful books about meaning and meaninglessness.

Living with no hope of love made the old man just too lonely, and one day he adopted a great tawny Rhodesian Ridgeback dog almost as big as a small pony. He had heard these dogs could fight huge African lions. He even heard that one Rhodesian 9/11 search-and-rescue dog named Shep was a direct descendant of the first Ridgeback that ever lived, a brave animal named Tsavo.

He named the dog Mr. Brown, and they became inseparable. Mr. Brown's tireless taste for exploring breathed new life into the old man. They journeyed for weeks at a time deep into the hills and mountains. At night by the firelight, the old man would sometimes weep, remembering his lovely wife. Whenever the old man's tears started to fall, Mr. Brown rested his strong head on the man's lap and made strange houndtalk that sounded remarkably human.

"Your beloved wife's energy is approaching, so be super-cautious now. That great big generous heart of yours is too easily fooled."

The old man remembered his wife had said the same thing and wondered how Mr. Brown knew to say that.

Mr. Brown enjoyed the circus, too. He sniffed a million enticing smells of exotic animals from strange lands, but one day he stopped sniffing and sat bolt upright when they reached the organ grinder's booth. There on a red-curtained stage stood a charming and flirtatious girl monkey named Beauty. She wore a bright-blue skirt, a shiny yellow taffeta blouse, and a tall-feathered cap tied to her round little head with a silver bow. Beauty acted like the old man was her long-lost love. She strained at the end of her leash, reaching out to him with her thin, hairy arms, chattering affectionately.

"My friend, my sweet! Oh, I have missed you so! Where on earth have you been?"

The old man rewarded her affection by offering a bright gold coin. Beauty snatched it up, tossed it high in the air, and caught it behind her back without even looking. The organ grinder said Beauty could perform marvelous tricks and if the old man would come back every day with gold coins, she would perform for him. The old man smiled while Mr. Brown lifted his leg and urinated at the organ grinder's feet.

The next day, Beauty performed her first trick. She jumped ten feet straight up into the air, flipped over twice, and landed standing upside down on the little monkey fingers of her right hand. The old man gasped with joy and gave her two coins instead of one. The organ grinder told the old man that tomorrow's trick would be even better and that he could show his appreciation by giving Beauty more gold. The old man crawled into bed that night too excited to sleep. Mr. Brown nestled up against him and kept an eye out for any approaching bad dreams. The old man slipped into a deep slumber with one arm lying over the great dog's broad neck.

On the second day, the organ grinder shooed all the other circus customers away so Beauty could do a daring private trick for the old man. It was more than ten times better than the twirling upside-down handstand from the day before. Beauty pulled a huge red banner out of her left ear and waved it back and forth faster and faster until it crackled like fireworks and lifted her into the air. Then a brilliant rainbow of yellow, blue, and red shot out of her forehead and formed a bridge to the shiny bronze star on top of the tallest big-top tent. Beauty danced back and forth on the edge of the rainbow, singing bits from famous love songs until she ran out of lyrics and came back down to her stage.

The old man gasped in astonishment again and gave Beauty three coins. Beauty reached out her tiny brown hands, took one of the old man's hands in hers, and stroked his palm softly. Then she kissed his fingers and made sweet chittering sounds. The old man's heart swelled, and the organ grinder smiled. Mr. Brown was still no great fan of monkey tricks.

Every day for a week Beauty's tricks grew more amazing and daring. She ran into the lion's cage and sat in the beast's mouth playing a tiny harmonica. She pulled the giant Burmese python out of its cage by the tail, tucked its tail into its mouth to form a huge scaly hula hoop, and rolled it right across the promenade into the ringmaster's private tent. She shaved off half of the bearded lady's hair with a gold razor and decorated the other half with silk ribbons.

One morning the organ grinder said Beauty was too tired to do tricks. The little animal only danced a half-hearted jig with her shoulders slumped and her eyes cast down. Her friendly, excited chatter had disappeared. She just frowned when she held out her cup. The old man wished Beauty would say something, but she was stone silent. He rubbed her head softly and put four gold coins in the cup to cheer her up. He walked home worried about his little friend, with Mr. Brown trotting dutifully at his side.

On the fourth day Beauty barely even moved. The organ grinder had to tug at her leash to get her to stand up. She just hunched listless on the stage. The old man patted her softly on the head and offered great care.

"What's the matter, my dear little friend? Why are you so sad? You are my sweet friend, and I want to help."

The organ grinder smirked and reminded the old man that Beauty was only a monkey and certainly didn't understand a word of what he was saying. The old man's supply of coins was running low but since he was so enchanted by the little animal, he dropped a half-dozen more in her cup.

On the fifth day Beauty could do nothing but lie asleep in the shade. The organ grinder told the old man that special monkey medicine would make the little girl perky again. A wild-animal trader could supply it the next morning, but only for a large sum of gold coins. It cost more coins than the old man could carry in his pockets, but he didn't think twice. He had to save Beauty. He prayed for her all night long and at dawn the next morning took the last of his gold coins from a carved rosewood box he kept hidden in his attic. He put them in an old leather bag and rushed back to the circus as fast as he could with the heavy bag thudding against his sides and the loyal Mr. Brown jogging along beside him.

When old man reached Beauty's tent, the organ grinder stood right there with a grim look. He said Beauty had died during the night. The old man's heart froze, and tears ran down his cheeks. He bit his lip so he wouldn't cry.

"Oh, no! Not again! Why does everything I care for have to die?"

He stared up at the sky, wondering at this latest twist of fate, but felt relief because Mr. Brown was a love he could trust.

The organ grinder did not seem to care about the old man's grief. He leaned forward and in a nonchalant voice said the best solution was to use the rest of the old man's gold coins to buy a new monkey and train it to perform. He reached out in a flash to grab the leather bag, but Mr. Brown erupted with ferocious growls, leaping forward and snapping at his hands with his formidable huge white teeth. The old man fell backward onto the hard ground, clutching his coin bag. Mr. Brown snarled menacingly at the organ grinder, who just kept talking.

"Wait a minute! We can get a new one! She was just a monkey. Just a stupid animal. It's not like she was anything special. They're a dime a dozen!"

The old man stood up slowly and dusted the dirt from his clothes. He thought about punching the callous organ grinder in the nose, but decided not to since he was more of a hopeless romantic than a fighter. Then he felt Mr. Brown nuzzling and pushing at his legs, which obviously meant it was time to go home. He put his coin bag deep into his coat pocket, took Mr. Brown's leash in hand, and the pair started the long walk home.

As they approached the house, the old man was still wiping away his tears over Beauty. He was daydreaming about her marvelous tricks and her sweet monkey chittering when all of a sudden he heard the faintest whisper of a very unusual voice. He perked up his ears and wondered if Mr. Brown could be making a different kind of houndtalk than he ever had before. Instead of the strange half-animal-half-human dog sound, something tenderly musical filled the air. The old man's heart skipped a beat, and his breath caught in his chest as he looked down at his loyal dog in disbelief. Mr. Brown met the old man's gaze and love poured out of his large golden eyes. In that instant, with their gazes locked, the old man recognized the sound. It was the same ballad his long-lost beautiful wife used to sing about the sweet, enchanted love they'd shared so many years before. Yet she was nowhere to be seen.

The old man froze, hypnotized in disbelief, as Mr. Brown's sinewy body began to sway to and fro in time with the melody. Like a slow-motion ballet dancer, he rose on his two hind legs until he stood straight up. His thick, feral head and prominent muzzle slowly melted away to reveal the soft rosy cheeks, kind eyes, and delicate pink lips of an angel. His sturdy forelegs and muscular haunches softened into two delicate arms and two svelte feminine legs as smooth and white as alabaster.

The bold, arrow-shaped ridge of hair that marked Mr. Brown as a pure Rhodesian Ridgeback came alive as flowing blond locks cascaded gently over the soft white shoulders and down the back to the narrow waist of this miraculous new being. The old man clamped his eyes shut tight in disbelief, hoping this was a real miracle and not just the hopeful fantasy of a broken heart. When he could wait no longer, he opened his eyes wide. There stood his long-lost love, reborn as living proof of the power of enchanted love. Mr. Brown's heavy leather leash dropped from her shoulders to the ground, and she stepped over it with small bare feet, reaching for the old man's hands.

"Here I am, my love. I told you I'd come back. I'm glad you waited. Let's go home."

Far away on the wild African savannah, bull elephants as tall as grey mountains rose up on their hind legs and trumpeted, and great tawny lions stopped still in the grass.

Mister Brown on his third birthday, April 30, 2015
Photo by Vic Sibilla

MICHAEL HOFFMAN is a doctor of addictive disorders (Dr. AD) and holds a Master's Degree in counseling psychology from the Pacifica Graduate Institute. He is a Vipassana mindfulness meditation teacher trained by Shinzen Young of Vipassana Support International. Hoffman has also earned his master hypnotherapist certification from the International Hypnosis Federation. *Ridgeback Tales* is dedicated to American Kennel Club Champion CH CJS Mister Brown HPK Tropaco CGC, a proud descendant of Tsavo. Hoffman's books, stories, and magazine articles include *Life After Rehab, The Thirsty Addict Papers – Spiritual Psychology for Counselors; The Blame Story, and Mind on the Run*. He first graduated from the University of Missouri School of Journalism and has received the Public Relations Society of America's top Protos Award for Excellence in Trade Journalism. He also contributes regularly to the international literary website *HelloPoetry*. He has practiced professional counseling in Dana Point, California, since 2003 with emphasis on mindfulness, Jungian depth psychology, mythology and Buddhist practices for the relief of anxiety, depression and obsessive-compulsive problems caused by materialism and decay of spiritual and environmental values.

75680681R00020

Made in the USA
Lexington, KY
18 December 2017